# THE UNICORNS WHO SAVED CHRISTMAS

by Mary Winn Heider

Illustrated by Christian Cornia

RP|KIDS
PHILADELPHIA

Running Press Kids
Hachette Book Group
1290 Avenue of the Americas, New York, NY 10104
www.runningpress.com/rpkids
@RP_Kids

Printed in China

First Edition: October 2020

Published by Running Press Kids, an imprint of Perseus Books, LLC,
a subsidiary of Hachette Book Group, Inc. The Running Press Kids name and logo
is a trademark of the Hachette Book Group.

The Hachette Speakers Bureau provides a wide range of authors for speaking events.
To find out more, go to www.hachettespeakersbureau.com or call (866) 376-6591.

The publisher is not responsible for websites (or their content)
that are not owned by the publisher.

Text written by Mary Winn Heider
Print book cover and interior design by Frances J. Soo Ping Chow

Library of Congress Control Number: 2019938169

ISBNs: 978-0-7624-9569-6 (hardcover), 978-0-7624-9570-2 (ebook),
978-0-7624-7009-9 (ebook), 978-0-7624-7008-2 (ebook)

APS

10  9  8  7  6  5  4  3  2  1

For Ruby—M.W.H.

To my "Santa Clause fan number 1" Tommy,
and to my "Santa Clause little helper" Erika—C.C.

Everything at the North Pole Unicorn Troop Headquarters
should have been perfect.

Peaceful.

Pulchritudinous.***

*Pulchritudinous* means "beautiful."
**Unicorns can be a little extra.

But it was not peaceful.
The North Pole Unicorn Troop was having
a problem. A loud problem.
Somebody was banging on their door.

The members of the North Pole Unicorn Troop discussed the problem. No one wanted to get chicken pox.

On the other hoof, maybe it was just somebody *named* Chicken Pox.

On the other, *other* hoof,
no one knew anyone named Chicken Pox.

On the other, other, *other* hoof, it was official Unicorn Troop rules
to help when help was needed.

So the unicorns opened the door.

"*You!*" gasped the unicorns. "Why—you're *Santa!*"
"I sure am," Santa said.

The unicorns immediately fell asleep.
All of them. At once.

"Hmm . . ." said Santa. "What exactly is happening?"

"We're pretending to be asleep," one of the unicorns whispered. "Everybody knows you don't get presents if you're awake when Santa comes."

"Ho ho ho!" said Santa. "Actually, that's not scientifically true. But if something isn't done soon, no one will get any presents tonight!"

This was serious. This required cocoa.

Once everyone had a mug, Santa explained.
His reindeer had gotten chicken pox. Even Rudolph. They had fevers and
were quite itchy. They certainly couldn't pull the sleigh tonight.

Santa had tried to find substitutes.

But the sleigh was magical.

Not just anybody
could pull it.

And so far,
**NO LUCK.**

The members of the Unicorn Troop
could not believe it.
How terrible! Christmas would
have to be canceled.

"And so," said Santa,
"I've come to ask you,
the North Pole
Unicorn Troop . . .

. . . if you would try
to pull my sleigh tonight?"

Them? Help Santa?
Absoposilutely!

But then:

Hic!

Hic!

Oh.

Oh dear.

Too much cocoa.

Too much excitement.

Too much . . . *pressure.*

Maybe they just weren't cut out
for this sort of thing.

"Well," said Santa,
"let's give it a whirl anyway."

On the way to Santa's workshop, the unicorns tried every possible cure for the hiccups.

Soon, it was time.
The North Pole Unicorn Troop
hoped they were ready.
They hoped they were enough.
They hoped they would be perfect.

Hic!

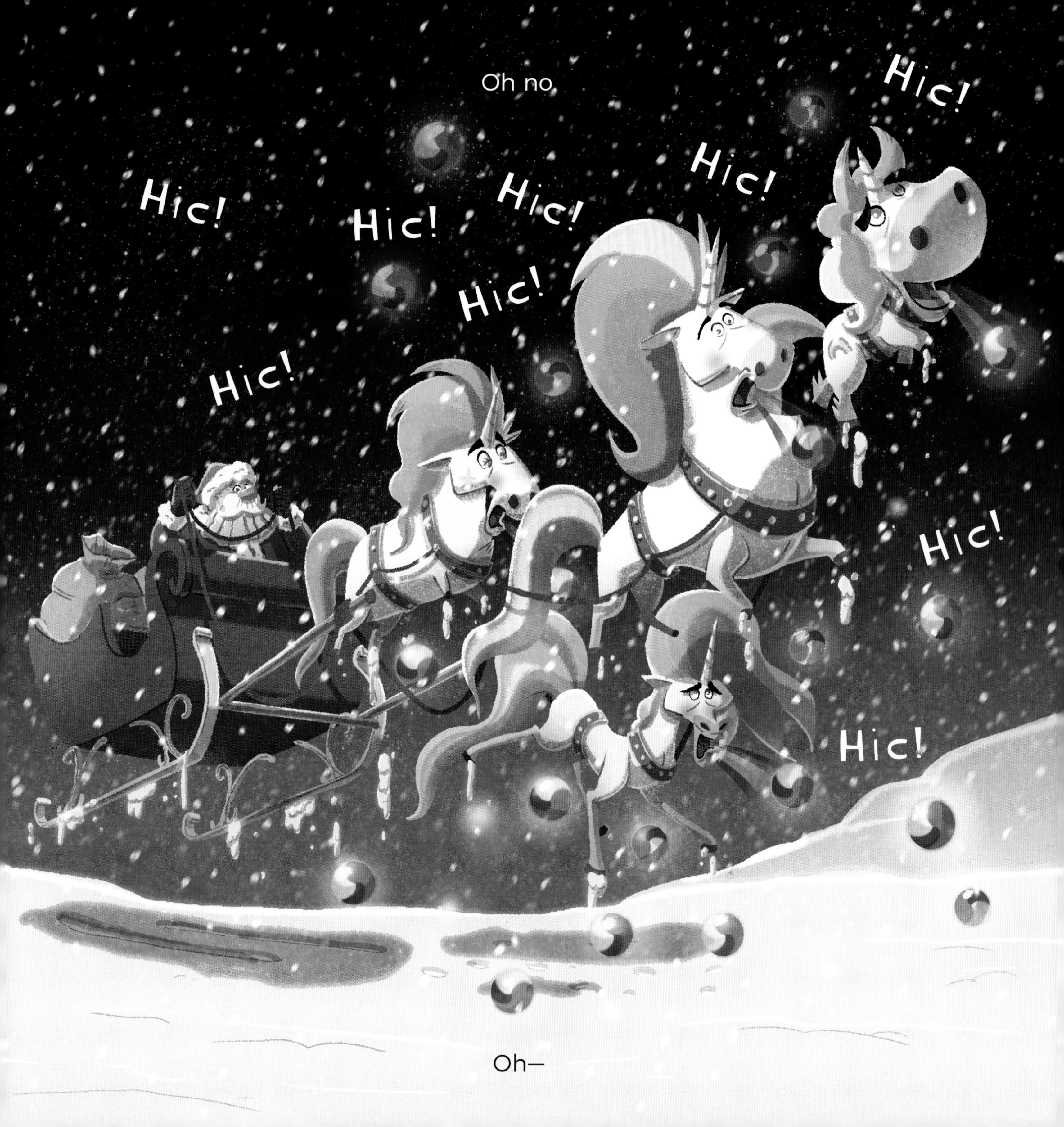
Oh no.
Hic!
Hic!
Hic!
Hic!
Hic!
Hic!
Hic!
Hic!
Hic!
Oh—

Oh!

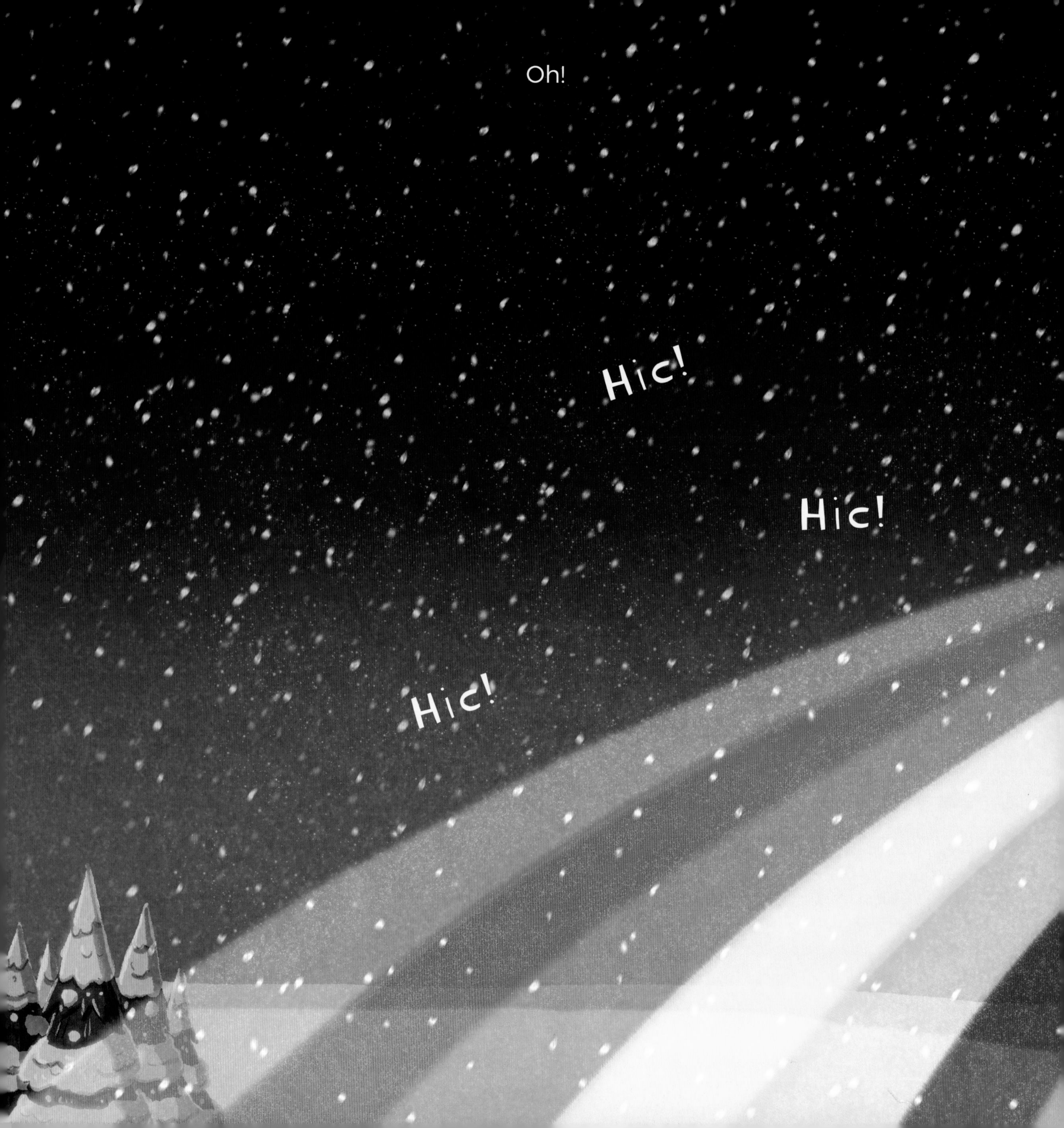

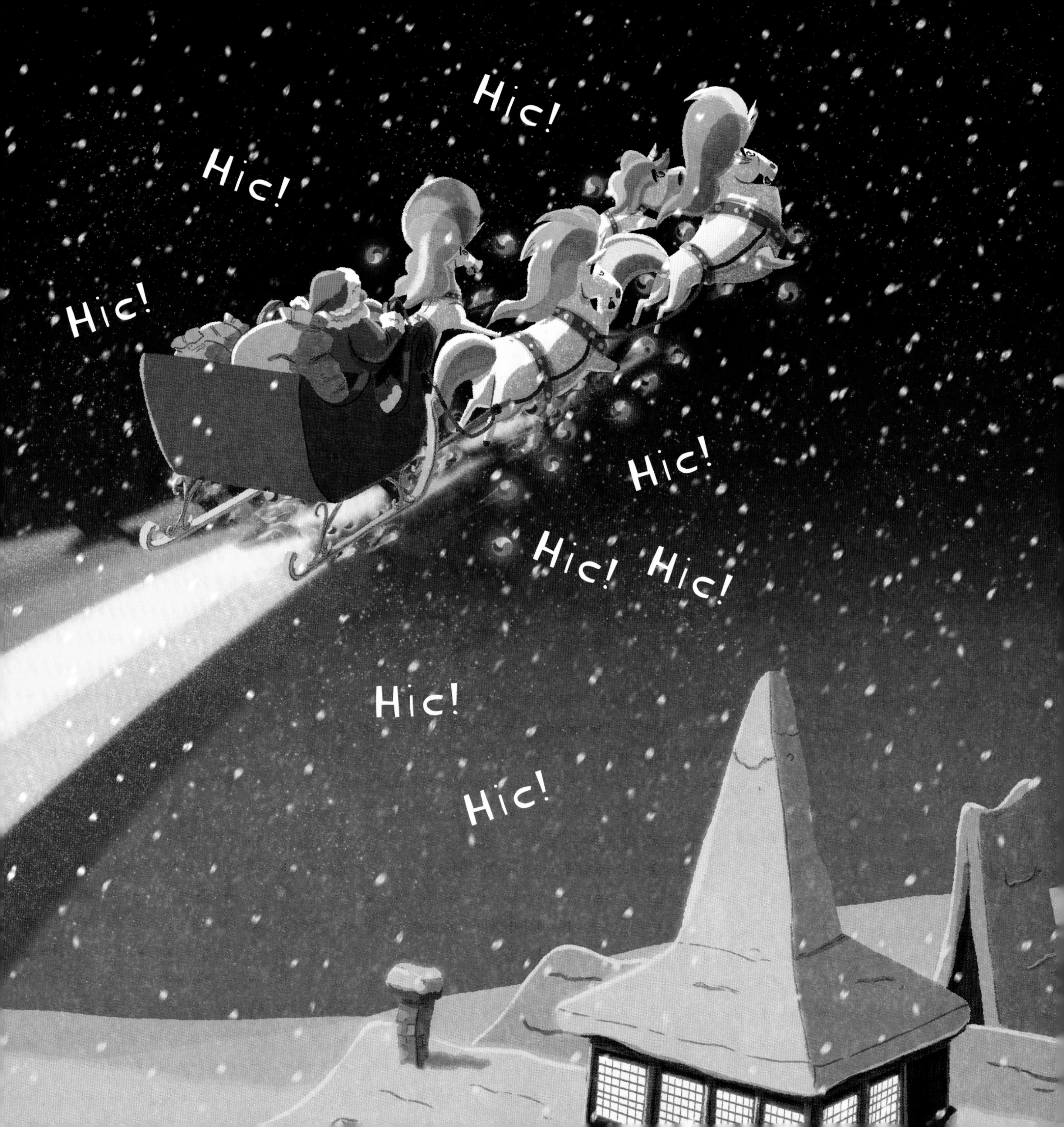
Hic!
Hic!
Hic!
Hic!
Hic!
Hic!
Hic!
Hic!

*Still means beautiful.
**Even when they're being reindeer, unicorns are a little extra.